It All Changes Now

Now

AMY LAURENS

OTHER WORKS

SANCTUARY SERIES

Where Shadows Rise
Through Roads Between
When Worlds Collide
The Complete Sanctuary Series

KADITEOS SERIES

How Not To Acquire A Castle

STORM FOXES SERIES

A Fox Of Storms And Starlight

SHORTER WORKS

Darkness and Good
Dreaming Of Forests
It All Changes Now
Of Sea Foam and Blood
Trust Issues

NON-FICTION

How To Create Cultures
How To Create Life
How To Map
How To Theme
How To Write Dogs
The 32 Worst Mistakes People Make About Dogs

Find other works by the author at
www.amylaurens.com/books/

It All Changes Now

AMY LAURENS

AUSTRALIA

Print ISBN: 978-1-922434-05-0
eBook ISBN: 9781393414056

www.inkprintpress.com

National Library of Australia Cataloguing-in-Publication Data
Laurens, Amy 1985—
It All Changes Now
108 p.   cm.
ISBN: 978-1-922434-05-0
Inkprint Press, Canberra, Australia
1. Fiction—Short Stories (single author) 2. Fiction—Science Fiction—Collections & Anthologies 3. Fiction—Fantasy—Collections & Anthologies

Summary: Tossed across the multiverse, two enemies must make peace if they wish to return to their own lives.

First Edition: November 2020

Cover design © Inkprint Press.

For Skribs, Akash, Fin, Indra and Alissa.
Love you guys <3

With immense thanks to LB, Kerryn, Clare.
These stories are better because of you.

Contents

The Multiverse May Burn

"THAT'S ENOUGH." THE JUDGE, IN HER STYLISED white wig and long navy robes, didn't shout, but she didn't need to. Her gaze—not baby, not cornflower, not sky, but rather poison-dart frog, or cavernous ice, or man 'o war—over the top of her black-rimmed glasses was severe, the gaze of a woman who'd seen far too many trouble-makers in her life for even a molecule of sympathy to remain in her blood.

Alissa shivered. Before, she'd thought that maybe, if she'd come in with a good enough story and a water-tight argument, she might have had a chance. But that look from the judge brokered no compromise, and Alissa looked quickly away, studying the flecks of black in the white-marble floor tiles.

Tiny specks of silver shone, and for a moment Alissa thought that maybe they represented hope amid the black-and-white of the justice system. But that, surely, was too much to assume; the room stank of bleach so strongly they might as well have advertised, 'One courtroom, clean of germs and mercy both.'

Stomach twisting, Alissa raised her gaze to stare at the walls instead, more uncompromising white, except where the recording screens—panels as tall as she was, as wide as her arm-span—interrupted them.

Three of the viewing screens were currently in use. From one, a severe-face man with salt-and-pepper hair and deep, deep lines in his dark skin frowned down at her. In another, the cyborg Natia Alchamp narrowed their hazel eyes, lightly-tanned fist clenching in front of them on the dark-wood desk they sat behind, occasional flares of colour coalescent around their head as they used their implant to access the multiverse.

And in the third…

Alissa swallowed heavily.

In the third, the most beautiful man she'd ever seen sat scowling at her, dark eyes full of something she could only assume was hatred. Two long, red scratches puckered his brown cheek and at the sight of them again, Alissa's stomach clenched, adrenalin punching through her system.

She could taste that blood in her mouth, metallic, sweet, and if anyone here thought she would ever be sorry for what she'd done, they had another thing coming.

She'd die first.

Literally, and they would be the ones to kill her.

Which, damn it all, it wasn't her *fault*. *They* were the ones who'd fed her mother Rapunzel in the first place, hoping for yet another super-powered child to join their ranks.

So how was it Alissa's fault if things had gone slightly wrong—assuming a spontaneous genetic mutation could be considered 'wrong'?

"It is obvious that you are as stubborn as you are articulate," the judge continued, as a school teacher disciplining an unruly child might. "But your arguments are irrelevant. The fact of the matter is that you not only possess the forbidden blood magic, you actively chose to use it on this man."

Alissa's nostrils flared. Curse Hannah. Curse the witches. Curse everyone involved with her birth—and most of all, herself. Alissa drew in a steely breath, the unforgiving bleach filling her awareness.

Well, so would she be. Unforgiving, resolved, and devoid of mercy. If they were going to sentence her to death for possessing a talent she hadn't asked for, didn't want, then by the Clans she'd go down swinging and take them all with her.

She snorted. Folded her arms. Raised her chin and stared back at the fair-skinned woman who thought herself worthy to lay judgement on this matter.

The judge narrowed her own eyes in return. "Well then, Alissa Fortuna McAlister. You have brought this fate upon yourself. You have admitted to wielding blood magic in an act of aggression against another human being, as if possessing the red magic wasn't bad enough, and we have seen recorded evidence that your magic glows red instead of blue, as it ought. You know the penalty for this is death."

Adrenalin pulsed again, this time with a sour squirt of acid in the back of her throat. Alissa coughed, trying to swallow away the burn.

This was it, then. This was the end, and she'd take them all with her—

She felt both magics, the sanctioned blue and the unsanctioned red, rising in her body, one cold and sharp like a migraine, one hot and tingling like pins and needles, a metallic taste rising in the back of her throat like blood, if blood were copper-blue instead of iron-red.

She couldn't do anything about Raiden, who'd dobbed her in and thus effectively signed her death warrant himself, and that... well, that pissed her off, to be honest.

But the judge was going to be sorry.

"*Unless.*" The judge pursed her blue-painted lips, so bright they made her skin seem pale as death, so bright they outshone her gleaming eyes.

"Someone will speak for you, and agree to complete a Multiverse Trial."

Alissa snorted, loudly.

Movement caught the corner of her eye. The older man, shifting restlessly.

In stark contrast, Raiden sat immobile, eyes wide with… something.

Joy, they ought to be wide with joy; he was getting what he wanted. So why wasn't he glad?

And then his mouth moved, and Alissa could have sworn she was dreaming but for the cold of the pew seeping into her thighs and the persistence of the bleach-stink and the fact that, even in her wildest of dreams, Alissa could never have made him say what he said:

"I'll do it."

Alissa stared. Realised her mouth was hanging open. Glanced surreptitiously at the judge and realised her mouth was hanging open also.

"Raiden," the judge said, voice suddenly warmth and concern and familiarity. "Are you *sure*? Are you even a compatible sponsor?"

He nodded—and this time Alissa knew exactly the expression he was wearing: barely suppressed terror.

She rocked back. But he… But *why*? And… What? Somehow, in the space of two long seconds, she'd lost the thread of reality.

"There is no out once you agree," the judge said urgently to Raiden. "I must urge you to reconsider."

Raiden shook his head, sallow-faced—but the terror had died down, leaving something determined in its wake. "I'll do it.

"So help me." The judge flipped her hands up in the air. "Fine. Let the record show that Raiden Ondrej Baník has agreed to sponsor Alissa Fortuna McAlister in a Multiverse Trial. You are one lucky son of a bitch," she added to Alissa. "You know how many times someone has agreed to this before?"

Mute, Alissa shook her head. She'd be shocked if anyone had *ever* agreed, because first of all, the Trial was a relatively new invention, made possible only because of Natia Alchamp's multiverse chip in the last century and a half.

And second of all, the Trial itself.

It was designed to prove that the person who'd been sentenced to death could—*should*—be saved, that their continued existence wasn't contradicting a fixed point in time. And to prove that, the convicted and their sponsor would be flung out, using the multiverse chip, across every accessible universe to see what would happen.

Wrapped in alternate bodies, names, identities, unable to remember their past lives, either they wouldn't find each other, and nothing would happen, necessitating a rematch—or they *would* find each other.

And if they found each other, either nothing would happen, thus proving that the convicted's continuing presence in their own universe was not a threat—or else the multiverse would burn.

The Witches did not grow to take over the literal universe and begin stretching their superpowered fingers beyond by playing nice.

"Two," the judge said, holding up two fingers. "Two times, a sponsor volunteer. The first time the convicted person died in every universe and the whole adventure changed nothing. The second time…"

She narrowed her eyes, expression darkening. "The second time, both sponsor and convicted died in every known universe. Including, once they were retrieved, this one."

Alissa swallowed, nausea surging in her stomach. It wasn't her fault, she hadn't asked to be born with two magics…

And it certainly wasn't Raiden's, even though he'd been the one to call the authorities on her. In his defence, she'd terrified him out of his mind by throwing a possessed kangaroo at him like that, and amped up on both magics she'd been more than strong enough to overpower him, something she'd known the Captain of the High Witches' Council would never expect.

But in trying to protect her *other* secret, she'd outed this one, and although the other secret was humiliating, this was the one that was deadly.

And now, Raiden was probably going to die too. Fat lot of good she'd done, trying to protect him from her *other* secret.

"You don't have to do this," she said—or tried to say, her throat was suddenly bone dry.

But the judge sniffed. "Too late. The sentence has been pronounced," she said, gesturing to fourth and final screen behind her, where the unblinking eye of the Arbitrator watched, infinitely patient, infinitely aware—and infinitely unchangeable.

Even now, Alissa's sentence of three years in the multiverse was scrolling across the bottom of the screen on a dark blue tickertape, Raiden clearly noted as her sponsor.

A *compatible* sponsor.

Alissa's chest seemed to be missing something—her heart, her lungs, something.

It was hollow, either way.

"Alissa," Raiden said. "It's going to be okay. I'll find you."

Alissa pressed her eyes closed against the whirling, swirling chaos of the courtroom. "Yes," she whispered. "But what then?"

Because honestly, the multiverse burning was the least humiliating of the two options.

Because the other option involved the revelation of that other secret, the one she'd attacked Raiden to protect in the first place.

Because the truth was, she was in love with him. And given her background, and given his position as Captain, that was a secret that she'd assumed would only ever end in shame—his—and banishment—hers, for daring to be so presumptuous.

But he was a compatible sponsor, and that meant—

A navy-clad guard appeared in the doorway behind the judge's left shoulder.

"She will take you to Natia," the judge said, inclining her head toward the guard. "Go." And then, as Alissa passed by, "Good luck."

Alissa left the courtroom with her chin high. There was only one way to be a compatible sponsor for someone condemned to a Multiverse Trial: You had to love them.

And so. One secret had gotten her into this mess. Perhaps the other one could get her out.

So long as they found each other.

And the multiverse didn't burn in the process.

"I'll find you." Raiden's voice echoed behind her as the door to the courtroom slid shut, and Alissa smiled sadly in the dark.

"Yeah," she whispered to no one. "You probably will."

And knowing her luck, the multiverses would burn.

For The Last Time

THE SUN-WARMED TILES, A SMALL, OBLIQUE SQUARE just in the entrance of the kitchen, soaked through Arav's socks like a fairy-charm against the cold of the rest of the house. He closed his eyes, hugging his mug of tea and luxuriating for a moment in sunlight that hit him from the chest down, truly warm for the first time all week, since before... Since *before*.

Chimes sounded in front of him, and he narrowed his eyes to glare at the tiny, translucent creature hovering in midair like the beautiful, miniature mutant offspring of a dragon, a human and a butterfly, all lilac and peach and iridescence.

"No," Arav said. "No chance, not at all, no way, nuh uh, no. Not now, and furthermore, never, ever again." He scowled. "No."

The creature smiled wryly. "I take it you are disinclined to acquiesce, then."

Arav's grip tightened on his hot mug. "Correct. The answer's no."

"Ah." It sighed, but Arav saw the gleam in its eyes. "It's adorable that you believe you have a choice."

"I do," Arav said. If he narrowed his eyes any further, he'd be squinting. "He specifically said that. You know. Last time."

"Yes, well. This isn't last time." The creature raised two tiny lilac eye ridges at him. "And I've been instructed to tell you that if you won't agree, you won't get Sandy back."

Arav twisted his lips to one side, chewing on the side of his mouth and mentally calculating how much the long-haired ginger cat cost him in food, vet bills, and general annoyance each month.

He exhaled. Tough call, but, "Fine. Fine! Bring me back my cat, and I'll do it. But this is the last time, do you hear me? The *last time*." He punctuated the last with sharp stabs of his finger, and it would have had more impact if the creature he'd been threatening hadn't been about four inches tall, coloured like an escaped swirl of country fair fairy floss—with a hair style to match—and a face cuter than the proverbial button.

The creature waved a hand dismissively. "Yes, yes, the last time. Look on the bright side: the weather's forecast to be much warmer next week." The grin it gave was—to use a particularly apt expression, in Arav's opinion—*impish*.

Arav shut his eyes and brought his tea to his mouth. He took a sip—three sugars, nice and milky, just perfect, and deliciously *warm*—and savoured not so much the steaming warmth that suffused him, inside and out, as the complete and utter lack of *cold*.

Man, he hated snow.

And the only thing he loathed more than having to shovel his own driveway was hiking two miles into the birch-and-juniper woods with a heavy snow shovel to clear out the fairy's ring for them, because of course it wasn't some dainty little circle, no: it was nearly sixty feet across and it didn't matter how sweaty he got from shovelling, the ice got into his lungs and it took *days* to stop the coughing, and now he'd agreed to do it all over again just to get Sandy back, and the damned cat had better stop scratching up the carpet on his stairs and remember just how much he loved her because he was agreeing to be very, very *cold* again, and all for her sake.

"Are you well?"

Arav cracked open one eye.

The fae creature seemed genuinely concerned.

He'd be touched if he wasn't certain it was because the creature was worried about finding someone else gullible enough to clear out the fairy ring if something happened to him.

"I'm fine," he said, because he was, really—so long as he took his asthma meds religiously and stayed out of overly cold air.

Ha ha.

But anyway, the creature was right: next week it was supposed to get warmer, so this really would be the last time.

And if it didn't get warmer?

Well, he'd discovered you could buy genuine used horseshoes online these days, and he'd be buying three of them—one for each external door—as well as a crap-ton of daisies from the local hardware store.

Sandy would get used to being an indoor cat.

It was only four months until summer.

The Fire Pony

CANJIN GLIMPSED THE PALE PONY WITH THE FLAMING mane and tail for only a second before it disappeared into the gorse brush. Grinding his teeth, he nudged the flanks of his own creamy white mare—regular mane, ordinary tail—and leaned forward as she surged into a gallop across the tawny sweetgrass meadow.

Canjin squeezed his calves, pressing the mare for more speed, even as she skipped and leapt and dodged her way around the sporadic, butterflowered shrubs and occasional logs that seemed to have landed as if by magic in the midst of a field entirely devoid of trees.

Dammit, the fire pony was getting away. Again. And he was running out of time to impress his father sufficiently to be named heir to the throne.

Faster, faster, faster: he pushed his mare for more speed, and more, and more, the cold wind whipping at his face—

And before he registered, he was flashing through the gorse, into a copse of birches where a narrow stream cut through the grassland…

And there, there was the flaming pony, palomino coat glistening in the sunlight, the smell of fire and ash thick in the air.

Canjin's mare reared, nearly unseating him.

He rebalanced, snatched at his rope, swung…

The rope settled around the neck of the flaming pony, szzing under the strain of the heat, but holding. Canjin's fact split into a grin—and froze as he realised his mortal mistake. He'd been so focused on *catching* the pony, he hadn't prepared for *meeting* it.

And it was rearing, sharp silver hooves flashing.

His mare bucked and propped away.

The flaming pony followed.

Ash stung Canjin's eyes, the rope burned in his hands, and he gripped wildly at the saddle, trying to stay on, because if he fell, the flaming pony would trample him in an instant.

Let it go.

It was the only solution.

He ground his teeth. No one would believe him, that he had the pony captured and let it get away like this, when he was so close he could taste fire in his mouth, feel the heat on his face, on the backs of his hands.

But dying wouldn't work to earn him the crown; he'd learned that the hard way after Danin passed away.

Flames licked at his ear. The rope tore against his palms…

—Canjin tossed it aside.

He'd find some other way to impress his father.

If nothing else, he'd have impressive wounds on his hands to show when he finally made it home.

The flaming pony screamed once and vanished into the birches, taking with it the scent of ash and flame.

Canjin's mare danced a few steps before settling, ears flickering as she snorted and grumbled.

Canjin tried to gather the reins, winced, and gave up. Instead, he nudged his pony with his thighs. "Come on girl," he said, weary. "Let's go home."

Perhaps he wouldn't impress his father with a fire pony. But something was bound to work eventually. Until then, at least he was alive.

Only A Single Rivet

The salty ocean breeze tugged at Rhyder, an insistent intruder trying to claim her attention. But it might as well have saved itself the trouble; a tornado could be approaching and Rhyder would only register it dimly in the very corners of her mind, absorbed as she was in the spring and stretch of the steel racer galloping beneath her. Its footsteps pounded the sand and she stood in the stirrups as the beast raced along, as poised and as focused as though sitting in an armchair reading a riveting book.

And, indeed, she was reading: on the screen of her visor, numerical stats flickered past in a never-ending stream. Most of them she could dismiss without thinking, but there was one string in the code she was watching for, listening, for, practically holding her breath for, because when—*if*, she had to believe the tuning would come good this time—if it appeared again, she had only a split instant to leap from the back of the racer, dive roll in the cold, hard sand, and hope to goodness nothing important broke as the racer stumbled, then collapsed into pieces.

4369-10.

Crap.

Rhyder dove to the sand mostly on instinct. Pain shocked her shoulder as she landed, tucking and rolling just as she'd done countless times before.

She rolled to a stop, sat up spitting gritty sand—and ducked as the left flank of the racer flew at her, a curved and moulded sheet of metal roughly the size of an old-style ironing board.

Ow. There went her shoulder again, sparks of pain shooting down her arm into her wrist like a sparkler.

Cursing under her breath, Rhyder hauled herself to her feet and trudged to where the flank had landed, some ten metres away in a gouge of damp sand. Rhyder lifted it one-handed, tapped it—a hollow, metallic noise rang out—to loose the sand… and frowned.

This piece of flank was supposed to be fixed to the body of the racer by a series of complicated rivets that would be hidden from view once the racer was fully assembled. The pattern of the rivets mattered: a criss-crossing pattern helped spell a racer who would explode from the blocks, ideal for short sprints. A circular pattern indicated a long-closer, one who could conserve energy to the end and release it in a final burst that might—or might not—win it the race. And a wave pattern, a series of 'u's going up and down, up and down, indicated the most prized racer of all: the endurance racer, who could run on and on and on and on for days, without needing a rest or refuelling or anything.

The patterns mattered—and placing them precisely mattered most.

Rhyder ran a fingertip over the wave pattern that glimmered in the sunshine on the back of the flank piece—and on the single rivet that was misaligned by only half a millimetre, just enough to matter.

She smiled through a mouthful of hair that the salty wind had blown into her face. Glanced at where the racer's body had collapsed into the wet sand, right on the tideline where the waves swept forward and back, forward and back.

Normally, she'd be furious that she had to spend big money on yet another repair job.

But this time... This time, she finally had the answer to the problem that had been haunting the racer that was supposed to have been the best long-distance runner this side of the mountains.

Clutching the flank piece tightly, Rhyder fairly danced back to the body of her beast. It was a long, long walk home—but the thought barely registered, absorbed as she was by the mental calculations of how *this* time, she'd have the beast fixed right.

Failsafe

Finlay scowled as he reached his hand into the guts of the time machine where cords and wires dripped with snot-green goo. It stank as bad as it looked, like stagnant bog water and rotting fish.

He hated slimy things.

Half an hour ago, a thing which was not slimy but which he still loathed on principle had decided to cough its guts up on the time machine—really a glorified Harley Davison nestled in a series of intersecting rings, all mounted atop a three-foot metal plinth housing the time vortex, the one into which he was now reaching—and ever since, Fin had been attempting to clean up the mess of monster snot and slime said coughing had created.

Travelling into the future was supposed to mean cool tech and flying cars. Not genetically engineered monster-freaks that looked like Darwin had gotten heavily involved with a swamp man coughing up goo into the engine of your time machine and grinding the whole thing to a halt.

Fin wrinkled his nose as the stench of the monster mucous hit the back of his throat again. Gross. If he could just find the switch…

When Fin had built the time machine, he hadn't been stupid (transparently obvious, because no one stupid builds time machines in their garage in their spare time between university classes and bussing tables at the local café): he'd installed several failsafes, assuming that at some point or another he'd find the machine bogged—a natural hazard when it was time you were travelling through, and not space.

But by sheer ill luck, the monster snot had disengaged the safety shields around the first three failsafes—he'd tried those and nearly been electrocuted back to the twenty-first century. And so here he was, stuck up to the shoulder in time vortex (which felt like a severe case of pins and needles) and monster snot (which felt like sticking your head into a bucket of fish guts, only significantly less pleasant), trying to reach the final safety in the innermost depths of the engine.

And the problem was, he was navigating his arm through five-dimensional space to do it. He *knew* the failsafe was *right there*, three centimetres left and directly behind last Tuesday, but could he quite reach it? No, of course not.

And the fact that the monster snot was, in essence, his own fault, didn't make him any happier with the situation. How was he supposed to have known that the genetically engineered monstrosity had also been built with a failsafe, one that meant it would practically turn itself inside out the moment a human being declared it a threat?

Stupid monster. Stupid goo.

He couldn't reach the failsafe, which seemed to him to be a gross error of judgement, because what good was a failsafe if you couldn't reach it to ensure safety from failure? When Fin finally fixed this mess, he was going to have a good, stern talking-to with his earlier self. Assuming he could figure out a way to do that without blowing his past self's mind.

Fin shook his head. That was a problem for future!Fin (and possibly past!Fin). Present!Fin still needed to find a way to reach the safety.

Last Tuesday. Last Tuesday…

Fin narrowed his eyes—partly in thought, but also to be fair and accurate, partly because a glob of monster goo had just dripped down off the left foot peg of the Harvey and landed on his forehead. It was cold, it was wet, it was viscous, and it stank of fish guts—or, more precisely, monster guts… But it reminded him that last Tuesday, the last Tuesday before he'd finished installing the failsafe, had been the last Tuesday he'd actually gone fishing with his dad (he did like his dad, but he didn't like fishing, which was why that had been the last time).

Which reminded him that "last Tuesday" was not just a place, it was also an idea.

With one last, gargantuan effort, Fin stretched his arm into the depths of the time vortex, and for the first time in over half an hour, let himself breathe deeply.

The stench nearly had him also turning inside out with coughing—but the olfactory memory did the trick, and he felt the little switch behind his pinky finger in the depths of the time machine's engine. There. There was last Tuesday, and there was the switch behind it.

Fin flicked it, and the time machine's engine coughed to life, choking—as they all were—on monster mucous, but breathing, exhaling, sputtering, and then finally running smoothly nonetheless.

Excellent.

Fin wriggled his arm back into the present day, massaged it until the worst of the pins and needles desisted, and climbed back onto the bike, the taste of bog water thick in the back of his throat. Time to have a chat with his younger self about failsafes.

The time machine roared, then faded into nothing, leaving behind only a gleaming puddle of monster snot.

Under Forty-Eight Hours

Ashlynn frowned deeply at the scene out the window: a tall, spreading oak, its leaves waving in the gentle spring breeze, daffodils bobbing underneath, spreading their strong pollen scent—and the sky, deep, clear, cerulean blue.

Abhorrent. The lot of it.

Mostly because the daffodils weren't hers, the oak had made it very clear that it didn't like her, and the sky was devoid of the iridescence that would indicate an incoming unit, here to save her from boredom and solitude.

Oh, sure, everyone *said* the retreats were a reward, but Ashlynn knew the truth: this is where mages were sent to think about what they'd done.

She'd told Valeri she wouldn't last forty-eight hours in this place, and she didn't intend to turn liar now. If she could just find the dampener…

Of course, combing the entire holiday cabin floor-to-ceiling looking for a non-specific object that might be as small and inconspicuous as a pinhead might well take her longer than forty-eight hours. But she was confident she'd fully swept the bathroom and the bedroom in the thirty-one hours since she'd arrived, so it was here in the living room—or else the kitchen. She was hoping for the far-simpler-to-search living room, but her luck had not borne out well so far, so she wasn't holding her breath.

At least there was little in the way of distraction here. Even the old, musty scent of a kitchen that had seen more decades than Ashlynn had didn't dampen her concentration as she stood in the little living room that was really the same room as the kitchen, segregated only by the abrupt transition from dark grey slate to the warmer but just as dark grey carpet.

She dug her toes against it, grounding herself firmly. With her eyes closed, the springtime scents from outside seemed even stronger, drifting in on the slight draft that the barely-open kitchen window offered, the slightly bitter taste of pollen coating the back of her throat.

Push that aside. Focus.

Sense the threads of movement in the room: the air currents, swirling just a little; her own warmth, radiating out into the room; the little fern on the single, raw-wood shelf above the worn-but-comfortable grey couch.

Ashlynn squeezed her hands into loose fists then relaxed, then squeezed again, pumping the air as though testing invisible ropes that crossed through the room.

When she was finally satisfied that she had a fix on the precise movements of everything in the room—the sun now sinking toward the horizon though the kitchen window, the rays of the setting sun stretching long fingers all the way through to the living room to tousle Ashlynn's copper-brown hair in its practical, slightly messy bun—when she'd quietened her stomach's rumbling and stilled her thirst and blocked out every single sensation but the quiet threads of energy permeating the room, then, then Ashlynn spoke a quiet word into air now thick with anticipation:

"Ahrlee."

It was a nonsense word, one she'd invented herself as a conduit for the seeking spell, a delicate, subtle weave designed to detect even the slightest distortion in an area about eight generous paces across. And because it was subtle and delicate, because it took several long hours to gather in her mind—especially without access to her props, forcibly left behind to 'encourage' her to 'rest'—the dampener, an indeterminate object placed somewhere here in the cabin to prevent her from working any kind of magic, couldn't block the spell.

It was about the only spell the dampener couldn't block, and Ashlynn had designed it that way deliberately after a particularly nasty run-in with a warlock back in her early twenties. She'd be damned if she'd let herself be caught without her magic ever again.

And so far, in the subsequent thirty years, she hadn't.

And she was going to keep her word to Valeri, and get out of here in under forty-eight hours, and have serious words with Shivani until she squealed and told Ashlynn who it was that had recommended her for this 'retreat'.

Nothing.

Not a single disturbance in the living room.

Ashlynn sighed abruptly and opened her eyes. The aches and pains of her body, stiff from standing virtually motionless for the best part of four hours, clamoured for attention.

She needed to pee.

And eat, and probably sleep, but those were all trivial details compared to the knowledge she'd gained from that last spell: the dampener hadn't been in the living room, so it had to be in the kitchen.

A quick trip to the bathroom and glass of water from the tap later, and Ashlynn stood in the centre of the kitchen, bare feet cold on the textured slate floor as she twisted to one side, stretching out her hip muscles.

The kitchen was going to be trickier. Laced as it was with water and electricity and gas pipes, there were a lot of natural energies here to interfere, lots of extra information for her to wrap in her mind before the detection spell would work.

The bathroom had taken her five hours, and it was a third the size of the frankly over-ambitious kitchen. (The cabin slept two people max, unless you wanted people camping on the living room floor. Why, then, did the kitchen need to be the size of one found in a generous family home?)

But there was nothing for it. She'd just have to section it off, the floor space and back door portion first and easiest, then the bit of the bench under the window with the sink and the corner cupboards, and then the ample pantry and ridiculously huge oven with their accompanying bench space and the gas burner stove.

Ashlynn pursed her lips, shook her head at the architect who'd designed the place, whoever they were, and made the three steps to the back door to ensure it was locked. She slid the kitchen window shut all the way—it was nearly silent on its runners, must have cost a small fortune for quality like that—and hesitated with her fingers over the light switch.

Outside, the sky had deepened to the green of twilight, and to the right of the oak a handful of stars had come out. Sidus was particularly twinkly tonight.

Ashlynn smiled at the star and left the kitchen lights off. She'd have her eyes shut anyway, and turning the light on would only create more electrical interference for her to work around.

She settled her feet on the slate, drew in a deep breath of cool air that still tasted polleny, though now there was a bit of night damp in there, too—knees slightly bent so they didn't cramp up, tailbone tucked a little to protect her lower back, shoulders loose, dispel any lingering tension—

Ashlynn began.

Dawn's long, pink fingers were just stretching their way toward the western sky out the kitchen window from above when Ashlynn found the tiny disruption to the energy fields flowing throughout the room. Over by the stove, toward the teal-coloured splashback, something no larger than the head of a small, silver pin was causing a tiny distortion in the energies fields.

Eyes still closed, Ashlynn stepped slowly toward it, ignoring the stiffness in her joints, the pain as muscles that had held still all night were asked to move again.

She hissed as she bumped the bench—but her eyes stayed closed.

There, just… there. Her fingers, guided by the spell, found the back of the stove top, and there, behind the lip of it, in the narrow gap between stovetop and splashback, Ashlynn felt a tiny bump. "Gotcha," she murmured.

Deftly, she scratched at the spot. In the pale dawn light, a tiny spot of silver gleamed on her fingertip: the dampener.

Ashlynn's smile was all tooth and wild, vicious delight. Staring at the dampener, she paced stiffly back to the bedroom and, with one hand, felt about on the bedside table—some sort of rustic, hand-made driftwood affair—for her knife, the blue and silver one that glimmered like metallic opal.

Shivani hadn't wanted her to bring it.

Ashlynn had told her where the knife would reside unless she *was* allowed to bring it.

And now, with a surge of ferocious happiness, Ashlynn used it to crush the dampener, the glimmering metal crushing away the power of the spell even as the flat of the knife itself crushed the tiny silver bug.

The sensation of the dampener breaking was much like that old childhood trick of tapping one's fist on a friend's head and then slowly spreading one's fingers down as though it had been an egg that had been broken.

Ashlynn shivered. Grinned. Grabbed the handle of the small suitcase that she hadn't bothered to unpack.

And—

Wait.

Ashlynn's lips pursed in satisfaction as she let out a thread of power. The glass on the large photograph above the bed shattered, the idyllic, pastoral scene rendered askance.

Now she could leave. And in under forty-eight hours, too.

Ashlynn called up her power, wove the spell of vanishing in her mind—

And was gone, already plotting how best to make Shivani squeal.

The Reality Of A Teal-Green Kettle

It's a cold, sunny day, the kind of day where the sun seeps into your bones and makes everything alright, even though the air itself is brittle enough to snap, even though you can feel it like ice as it whispers in through your nose.

It's good. The solstice has passed, there are a few more minutes of daylight every day, and it's not miserable and cloudy like it was yesterday. You soften as you see the golden gleam of daylight peering around the edges of the blinds; it's not going to be another day like yesterday. It's not.

In the kitchen, surrounded by teal appliances that cost you way too much, kept company by a raggedly little bouquet of dandelions the neighbour's kid picked for you three days ago—some of them are drying out, but you won't toss them, not now, not yet—you boil the kettle for tea. The way the steam curls up out of the teal-green spout to dance in the sunlight reminds you of something, but you can't quite get a grasp on what. It's like mist over the ocean, or steam from a hot pool like that one time you visited Coromandel, or...

You sigh. It's like hopes and dreams that you cling to so hard that eventually they take shape as a teal-green kettle, and they're trying so hard to be solid despite everything that they leak ephemerality a little around the edges.

Only when you look at them too hard.

But the sun reaches the kitchen bench here, gilding your hands as you carefully spoon black tea—flavoured with cherry, this morning, you never drink black tea neat—into the stainless steel infuser. You balance it carefully in the top of the glass flask, and when the kettle summons you, you perform the ritual with care, watching as the water enters clear and drains into the bottom of the cylindrical flask gold-hued.

The water rises, rises, right to the top, and you set the kettle down, set the microwave timer for three minutes because even if you stand *right there* and stare at the tea the whole time, you know from experience you'll let it overbrew and it will get all bitter and brown, like you're trying to drink tree roots perhaps.

The flask glimmers beneath its own halo of curling, dancing steam, and in the golden-crisp morning light, it could be a potion, brewed to perfection attained through long years of practice—though in reality you only started drinking tea a year or so ago, the doctor thought the calming ritual might help you—and it would be so, so nice if it were a potion, a magical cure, one-and-done, instead of this mindless, unending slog.

The timer beeps.

You lift out the strainer by its little handle, so close to being too hot to touch. In a moment, you'll open the strainer so the tea can dry out—don't want another Mould Episode, especially not since your mother is planning to drop around on Sunday—but for now, the little hole-pricked canister can sit on the draining board by the sink, slowly seeping golden fluid.

A dash of full-cream milk; the space left by the canister is the perfect amount, for flavour, for colour, and for cooling the tea enough that you can taste a little sip right now, as the sun rises slowly, inexorable, stealing its promise of warmth from your kitchen. Already the light has left the sink.

You sip, and the warm liquid unfurls down your throat, and you smile, because today is not like yesterday, and you're going to tackle it, and even if you only get one thing done, it's a thing more than yesterday, and that is well.

As you leave the kitchen, the teal-green kettle continues steaming, a solid form that blurs around the edges... but it's real enough, and it's in your kitchen, and it's yours.

Dragon Theft

In the smoky darkness of the club's secluded corridors, Akash stared at the glimmering, writhing dragon. Through the dark, inch-thick iron bars in the dim mood lighting, the three-foot-long scaled beast was barely more than a few flashes of emerald green and the glint of a golden eye.

Akash's pulse pounded wildly nonetheless, his hands sweating inside his thin leather gloves.

Two minutes. Two minutes to pick the lock, bond the dragon, and get out.

The steady rhythm of the baseline from the club's dance hall thrummed through the walls, the black matte paint soaking up the gold light from the naked bulbs overhead. He couldn't be sure he'd hear footsteps if someone approached.

Teeth clenched, jaw twitching, Akash twiddled the lock on the cage.

The dragon hissed.

"Shut up," Akash murmured, glancing over his shoulder. He wasn't the only one here to steal a dragon tonight—just the only one who'd be successful, because Daniel was an arrogant idiot, and that vanilla mortal who'd broken in not five minutes in front of him was, well, a plain vanilla mortal, who obviously didn't know that the dragon would kill him as soon as breathe the second it got hungry.

The pin he was using to pick the lock snapped. Akash swore.

Sweat trickled down behind his ear as he stared at the snapped pin, wreathed in shadows.

Dark night. Now what was he going to do?

The dragon hissed again, smooching itself against the bars like a cat, scales glittering, glimmering, flashing and flickering.

All he needed was a second of skin contact.

Could he risk it? Could he do it, forcing his hand between the iron bars and holding it there long enough for the dragon to feed?

He shuddered at the mere thought of iron against his skin, burning, blistering…

The dragon hissed softly, a sound almost like speech.

And Akash straightened. Yes. Yes, to fetch back one of the Caged, he could do it.

He peeled the glove off, one finger at a time. Inhaled. Hesitated for a brief moment a breath away from the bars.

The dragon bared its teeth, sensing a meal.

Akash plunged his hand between the bars, biting back a scream. The dragon's fangs sank into his hand—blood, blood, blood—but it was nothing to the fire and burn of the iron.

Three.

Nine.

Fifteen.

Thirty seconds was enough, and he was nearly there, nearly…

The dragon gave a gleeful little cry and vanished in a puff of glittering green.

Akash reeled back from the cage, gasping. Cradled his burnt hand in his whole one. Sucked air through his teeth.

Something skittered up his arm.

He pulled back the loose sleeve of his crisp cotton shirt—and bared his teeth.

The dragon wound around his arm, seemingly embedded in his deep brown skin. It twined over and around and around and around, a glittering, glimmering, iridescent tattoo. It shifted itself, sliding up past the crook of his elbow. Hot breath tickled the back of Akash's neck.

He pulled down his sleeve. Grinned fiercely through the stink of mortal hallucinogens and the clumsy, primitive thrum of subpar mortal music. His hand throbbed—and it didn't matter, because he had the dragon, and now he was going home.

Hope In The Shape Of A Feather

THE DOOR—AN UNBELIEVABLY OPULENT AFFAIR, intricately carved with leaves and flowers, overlaid with accents of gold, a full nine feet tall—was unexpectedly cold, and for a moment as she grasped the golden knob, Athara wondered if it had been alarm-spelled. She held her breath and turned the knob anyway, adrenalin pounding, heart surging—but the door swung open on silent hinges, and no one came running to stop her.

Elasu had been right after all.

A sharp intake of breath.

He'd also said the Artifice was stored in a small drawer, and he was probably right about that, too. He just hadn't mentioned that the whole facing wall was *covered* in drawers, all different shapes and sizes, ranging from as small as the width of her palm to as wide as the length of her arm.

Gently, Athara closed the door behind her. The golden handles of the drawers glittered in the late afternoon sunlight from the tall, narrow window on her right, and for no other reason than that it was the shiniest, Athara grabbed the handle on a square drawer the size of her head, and tugged.

The drawer stuck.

She tugged harder.

It gave—and an alarm shrieked overhead.

Breath in her throat, Athara cast about the room. No space under the wall of drawers. Spindly desk didn't provide enough shelter. Behind the door? *Far* too much of a last resort.

Curtains it was.

Footsteps echoed down the hall outside as Athara rushed to the bottle-green curtains. Thank goodness they were voluminous, all pleats and heavy, velvety drapes, more than sufficient to hide herself behind.

The door clicked open.

The sun warmed Athara's back through the window—snoot, what if someone saw her from outside? Too late now, she couldn't move, could barely dare to breath as whoever it was that had entered the room closed the drawer Athara had opened with a little shhhh.

Athara's right foot was going to sleep. As slowly as possible, Athara readjusted her posture—and realised that the curtain didn't quite meet up with the wall at the edge of the window. Through the narrow slit, she watched as a youngish woman with severe eyebrows and a serious haircut frowned at the drawer wall.

Then, as if impulsively, the woman reached out for a drawer close to the middle of the wall—chest height, a little larger than a handspan across and half as tall. The drawer threatened to stick, but the woman whispered to it and it skipped free, and from inside the woman withdrew a long, crimson feather, broad and frondy.

Athara's eyes widened. Her fingers twitched at her sides.

Don't take it, don't take it, don't take it.

Fate, it seemed, was on Athara's side: the woman replaced the feather, shut the drawer, and with one last glance about the room, left.

Ten seconds. Twenty.

Two minutes. Three. Five.

Once she was absolutely certain the woman wasn't coming back, it only took a moment for Athara to slide out from her hiding place and retrieve the feather from its drawer. "Elatra haneh," she whispered so the drawer wouldn't stick, just as the woman had done.

The Artifice. Athara smiled in wonder at the soft, crimson feather in her hands. Was she imagining it, or did the scent of cinnamon linger faintly around it?

She bowed her head, pressed it to her face, inhaling deeply while still she smiled.

And then, it was a simple matter to tuck the Artifice away into the pouch at her hip, close the drawer, and leave.

The intricate, commanding golden door closed behind her, just as though she'd never been.

Finally, A Cryptid

THE THRUM OF THE SUBMARINE'S WARP ENGINES vibrated through Kiernan's feet. Three weeks, and still his teeth felt like they were constantly buzzing. Absently, he pressed his left fingers to his jaw to still it, while with his right hand he adjusted the sonar tracking. It'd all be worth it if he could just get the 'don back on the screen, just hold the signal long enough to get a really solid trace he could beam back to base.

But the tracking screen stayed dark, the intermittent bip of the radar marking off the seconds.

The radar screamed.

The control room erupted into frantic movement as Kiernan locked onto the signal and the navigators scrambled to course correct.

There, there ahead…

Kiernan actually stumbled back a step, because he didn't need the sonar anymore. There, *right there*, outside the viewing panel, lit by the ghostly lights of the sub, the megalodon hung in the water.

All he could see through the right viewing panel, as wide as his arm span, half as tall as he was: one great, unblinking eye.

This wasn't a megalodon as predicted: this was a monster of a different order of magnitude.

Frantically, Kiernan mashed keys, trying to beam the signal back through kilometres of water and even more kilometres of atmosphere and space. Catching the satellite from this deep had always been half the challenge of trying to find the giant shark that had surfaced three months ago, caught on indisputable footage from fifty-three smart phones off a commercial whaler.

The 'don nudged the submarine with its six-foot snout.

And Kiernan realised they'd made a terrible, terrible mistake. There had been two significant challenges, for sure: how to find the shark, and how to get the signal back once they did.

But they'd forgotten a third and critical difficulty: how to get back home. Alive.

The shark nudged the sub again.

"Sir?" The head navigator shot Kiernan a sidelong glance.

"It's still connecting, give it a second."

Three months, three months and ten long years hunting cryptids before that and here he was, about to realise all his dreams, and the damn signal wouldn't connect.

The shark nudged the sub a third time, more insistently.

Kiernan's pulse raced. Fifty fifty: either the shark would lose interest and disappear now… or the next nudge would be with its teeth. God knew, the sub was putting out enough electrical input to make it seem like a megalodon-sized turtle.

And the worst of it was, Kiernan wasn't sure which option would be worse.

"Sir!" The head navigator was staring fixedly at him now.

Kiernan swallowed. Stopped fiddling desperately with the signal's controls. Slipped his smart phone from his pocket, thumbed open the camera. Swallowed again. "When I say go," he said, voice low and hoarse, "burn it."

"Sir?"

Kieran glanced over at the navigator's puzzled face. "Away," he clarified. "We're going back."

The navigator gave a tight but satisfied nod.

"Three," Kiernan said as the shark's eye disappeared momentarily from the viewing pane. He held the phone up so it could record the view. "Two."

There, not much more than a murky shadow in the dark. No one would believe that.

"Sir!"

"Go!" Kiernan held the phone steady as the shark lunged, teeth the size of his two hands together bared. They flashed clearly in the submarine's lights as the high-powered sub shuddered almost immediately to full speed—and clipped the end of one of the sub's fins.

Metal broke off with a tortured groan—but the sub was dashing away now and the giant shark obviously hadn't liked what it had tasted. It didn't follow, and they didn't have the signal… but it didn't matter.

Kiernan collapsed into a seat, wiped sweat from his temples—and hit play on the perfect video on his phone, showing clearly the shark's giant, ser-rated teeth as they flashed past the viewing pane.

Ten years—and finally, he'd found a cryptid.

Blood Dragon

THE IRIDESCENT GREEN DRAGON TATTOO ON THE man's bicep bared its teeth, and the teeth glinted under the black lights of the club. The pounding rhythm of the bassline drilled into Anya's skull, and the stink of weed and sweaty bodies writhing against each other made it hard to think. But, gaze locked on the dragon's, Anya wove through the crowd anyway, determined not to let it get away again.

At the far edge of the dance floor, the man—muscled in a long, lean kind of way, mid-brown hair, eyes probably dark as sin in his tanned face, though it was impossible to really tell in this light—turned, winked, and vanished through a doorway he shouldn't have been able to walk through.

Anya ground her teeth and swore loud enough that the precious blonde girl to the right with the pigtails raised her eyebrows. Anya flipped her off and headed for the doorway.

Only it wasn't a doorway anymore, it was a door. A fairly standard door, matte black like the rest of the club's walls—and it wouldn't budge.

Anya swore again and ground her teeth. She tasted blood—and stilled.

Right. Blood.

The grin she gave was sharp-toothed enough to scare away the handsome little boy—maybe twenty, twenty-two—who was trying to catch her attention on the edge of the dance floor.

Good riddance.

Anya closed her eyes, concentrated on the sweet taste of blood on her tongue, and let her mental defences fall.

The club screamed around her, the thoughts and desires and hungers of a hundred sweaty, unprotected minds rubbing against her in raw agony.

She ground her teeth harder; she only had to bear it for a few minutes, then it would be all over and she could raise her mental shields again.

Somewhere in something that felt like the far distance, but which was probably only just outside the front of the club, in the dim stairwell that led to the night-blanketed street, something green sparkled.

Here, little dragon, Anya crooned. *Come taste my blood. Mmm, tasty blood.*

She rolled her tongue around again, trying to saturate her awareness with the metallic tang.

Something in the distance, or else quite close by, perked up its interest.

Yes, yummy blood. He won't give you blood. He doesn't know how to feed you. He doesn't know that you need blood to survive. And he won't listen to you, he doesn't know how. Go on. Try asking him for blood.

A silence, filled with the screeching, scraping cacophony of unprotected minds and heavy bass lines and the smell of weed and sweat.

No, no. Blood. Only blood.

A flare of hunger in the darkness.

Anya smiled. *See? He doesn't know how to listen to you. Come. Come back, and I'll feed you.*

Her heart pounded at the prospect, but it was a small price to pay to secure the dragon again.

Another split-instant pause, and then something roared in the darkness behind her eyes.

Anya jerked as something hit her with the force of a freight train. She stumbled, reeled, fought back a scream as something tore through the skin on her bicep and shoulder, like a hundred thick needles piercing every pore.

Breathing heavily, she propped herself against the wall by the new door and stared blindly out at the writhing crowd as they danced in the flashing lights.

Blood, blood, blood.

Yes, Anya replied wryly, glancing down to see the dragon spiralling and twining round and round and round her shoulder and upper arm in ecstasy under the surface of her skin. *Blood. Alright, that's enough,* she said, and bopped the glittering green dragon on the nose.

Blood, it sighed wistfully. But it stopped.

Gradually, the pain in Anya's arm dimmed to an ember glow.

She inhaled deeply, exhaled through pursed lips, glanced at the door. The door was going to be a problem.

But it was a problem for later.

Right now, she had to get this bloody dragon back behind locked bars.

The Fey Gain Entrance

Neon lights flashed red and purple above the club's dark stairwell, promising pain for any fey who entered. Jasmari cast them a scathing glance, rubbed the cold tip of her nose, and descended the four steps to the door regardless. Her nose wrinkled at the stench of the daisies, all shrubby in their terracotta pots, two to either side of the door. Next time, she was doubling her rates; she'd be lucky if she even got *in* to this place, never mind accessing the information her client had requested.

First things first, she told herself. One goal at a time. First, make it inside.

"I'm here for Nate." She jutted her chin up at the burly bouncer, all thick, bulging muscle and charmed dark leather and eyes too pretty for his face.

The bouncer snickered. "Nate don't see your kind."

Jasmari folded her arms tightly over her ribs and narrowed her eyes. "He'll see me. Tell him Princess Jasmine has arrived."

Bouncer-boy muttered something into his collar and, within seconds, his eyes widened and he stepped aside. Bowing low, he gestured her toward the door. "Your highness."

Convincing, if you hadn't seen the malicious grin.

And of course, he hadn't actually *opened* the door.

Jasmari steeled herself. Swore. Jaw twitching, she grabbed the handle—and choked back a scream as pain tore through her.

Beside her, the bouncer laughed, a guttural 'hur-hur-hur'.

Jasmari ground her teeth, nursing her hand and glaring at the still-closed door. *Yeah, come here and laugh. I'll knock your teeth into the dust and curse your bones to spiders.*

"Hey."

A soft, male voice made her swing to the right, scanning the shadowy corners of the stairwell. "Who's there?" Iron spikes, she sounded spooked.

The bouncer was still laughing. In a hot minute, she was going to knee him in the stomach just to make him shut up.

From the shadows resolved a man whose hard expression seemed at odds with a face fresh out of high school.

"Nate."

He nodded long and slow. "Your Highness."

From him, it sounded the way it should: genuine, respectful, a little warm around the edges.

Jasmari gathered herself, tilting her chin.

"I heard you wanted to see me. Please. This entrance is much more to your liking." He swept into a courtly little bow, gesturing into the shadows from whence he'd appeared.

Ah. A new, second door had been fitted. Interesting.

The bouncer was just about swallowing his tongue at the exchange—a fact that, luckily for him, Jasmari took sufficient satisfaction in that she didn't bother making him *actually* swallow his tongue, though with a flick of her fingers as she swept toward Nate, she did give him an itching rash in his groin that would last him the next seven days.

She smiled just a little as the stink of the daisies and the night-cold alley were swallowed by the barely-improved perfume of sweat and hallucinogens emanating from the doorway. Never mind double. For this, she should have charged triple.

But at least her first goal had been achieved.

Some Impropriety Expected

NOBODY SUSPECTED SKRIBS OF BEING AN ASSASSIN, and that was his strength. At six-foot-three with limbs that had never outgrown their gangliness and a smile too big for his face, people tended to assume he was still a harmless, good-natured kid.

To be fair, he was.

Except for the kid part. And the harmless.

Lorelei had been an assassin too, at least until her ascension to the throne five years ago. Five-foot-three, with blonde hair down to her hips in its braid and hands so tiny she had to wear child-sized gloves, people tended to assume that she was still a fragile, slightly-serious princess.

To be fair, she did tend to be serious.

Only now, she was a slightly-serious queen.

She'd never been fragile.

Skribs knew that, and loved it best about her; childhood friends, they had vowed to have each other's backs forever and all time—and just because she was now the queen, that hadn't changed a jot.

And so, as the courtiers in their metallic-thread finery, crystals in their hair and embroidery down their sleeves, pearls upon their fingers and iron-stars round their necks, all stiffened in shock in the palace's receiving hall, Skribs came immediately to attention.

He barely noticed the severed head that tumbled to the ground from the wooden box, delivered by an ambassador from the North.

It was a Northern ambassador: some impropriety was to be expected.

To be sure, Skribs noted the blood splatter upon the travertine floor that indicated the death was recent; mentally changed his map of the room to avoid that section in case the footing was precarious; added the ambassador to the list of people he'd sooner see dead than alive.

But he was busier staring at another man, across the far side of the hall, who alone seemed less horrified by the severed head than satisfied at Her Majesty's reaction to it.

Though—Skribs cast her a glance—Lorelei had not in fact reacted to it at all. Not yet.

She stood stock still, only the slight shift in light from the silver buttons and strips of braid across her formal coat showing that she breathed at all.

Skribs pursed his lips. He knew what followed a look like that, that moment of perfect stillness, and it was death.

But the man across the way was still staring at Lorelei, keenly, too keenly, and Skribs' senses were on alert, sensing danger.

Slowly, he began moving his way around the room, drifting with apparently aimlessness while the courtiers recovered themselves and began to murmur about the head, the young head, the head of Lorelei's cousin who'd not yet turned one-and-twenty.

The smell of blood was in the air, and it spoke some measure of Skribs' life thus far that the way it mingled strangely with the taste of wine in the back of his throat was actually somewhat familiar.

The other man was moving now as well, drifting just as Skribs was, circling slowly closer to Lorelei, his eyes still sharp, still keen, his narrow face pinched like a hawk.

Skribs smoothed down the flap of his coat pocket. The familiar lump of his favourite glass vial greeted his fingers.

Perfume, the smell of white rose and lily. It was a favourite amongst some of the courtly ladies right now, but he hated it; reminded him too much of his mother's funeral, where his sister had insisted on such a gaudy display of flowers that white lilies still interrupted his dreams with teeth and long, twisting tongues.

Skribs wrinkled his nose, kept moving.

The man was close, now, to Lorelei, staring hungrily as she motioned for her sword, unaware of his proximity as she focused on the Northern ambassador.

For a moment, Skribs' heart tripped in his chest. This wasn't the Lorelei he knew, to draw sword in front of everyone and strike the ambassador down. Did she mean for a war? They wouldn't win, not if it began like that, and…

Skribs, despite his training, couldn't help himself: like every single person in the room, he inhaled sharply as Lorelei lifted the sword to the side of her head, and with one clean swipe cut the long rope of her hip-length braid.

She held the blonde hair aloft, a hint of fury surfacing in her dark eyes.

Skribs' heart remembered how to beat; he exploited the moment to draw close to the hawk-faced man, who even now was reaching under his coat as though for a weapon.

So. Lorelei *did* mean to start a war, did she? For that was what the severed braid signalled, and the ambassador clearly knew it—and just as clearly had not expected it.

Not like that. Not from her, the young, small, fragile Queen who championed peace.

Skribs clamped his hand firmly around the wrist of the hawk-faced man just as he drew a wicked knife from its sheath, and watched as only a few paces away, the ambassador's face paled in response to Lorelei's declaration of war.

Lorelei leaned in close to the ambassador, somehow seeming to loom over a man who had half a foot on her in height.

Skribs smiled grimly. Good for her.

He knew she'd be disappointed. Knew she'd wanted to do this the bloodless way—that was what the last five years had been all about, trying to prove that the old ways, the ways of blood, weren't needed any more. But woe betide those kings who had crossed her path now. Skribs had no doubt whatsoever that she'd slaughter them all.

And he'd be there, beside her, or more likely behind her, watching her back and fighting with the best of them.

But first, he was going to take out this piece of trash.

He hauled on the wrist of the hawk-faced man, jerked it upward and pinned him. Skribs leaned to the man's ear, and smiled. "No one touches the queen," he whispered, a salty breeze full of the promise of ice.

The little vial slipped from his pocket, and it was a matter of nothing to palm it under the man's nose, to watch as the man's eyes went wide with shocked recognition—to release him and watch as, horrified, the man went stumbling away, pushing courtiers aside in a most unseemly fashion.

So they were going to war against the North, were they?

Well. There went one fewer Northerner to threaten the queen.

Skribs tucked the recapped vial back into his pocket, and slowly drifted from the hall. Lorelei would handle the fall out of her declaration of war just fine, and in about five minutes—or less, depending on how good the hawk-faced man's metabolism was—Skribs would have a corpse to clean up.

It might have been a touch blasé to whistle as he left the receiving hall—but Skribs was just a lanky, good-natured boy, and some impropriety was to be expected after all.

Elsewhere

Probably, the small blue fairylights hanging around the outdoor bar in the corner of the overly large yard were supposed to lend a magical air to the party. To Indra, however, they merely looked tacky, a visible reminder that this was not some island paradise, but rather a lawned backyard with fruit trees espaliered around the fences and imported sand grounding the fake palm trees by the bar.

Also the bass was too loud. Her brother would have done a much better job DJing.

As she drifted through the crowd, the scents of pine and coconut, cheap men's deodorant and floral perfume clamoured for attention, only to be briefly swept away by a breath of air coming in from the ocean that lay some thirty kilometres east.

Indra inhaled the salted breeze appreciatively. The beach was infinitely preferable to this squalid gathering—especially on a moonlit night like tonight: the way the moon silvered the waves made her breath catch every time, and the sand squea-king under her footsteps was refreshingly cool, so fine it was almost soft, and on nights like tonight where the moon was full and the phosphorescence came out to play, Indra could almost believe there was magic in the world after all.

But she'd promised Denali she'd come to his birthday party, and so, despite her longing to be elsewhere, here was where she was.

Indra sighed. Probably, she should grab a glass of something, at least for appearance's sake. Sur-reptitiously, she checked her phone. Nine-oh-six. Another hour *at least* before it'd be polite to leave.

She sighed again, and drifted closer to the six-foot-long wooden bar that gleamed and glimmered in the soft mood lighting—

And tilted her head. Something had been tick-ling the edges of her mind since she'd arrived, something she was missing.

It was the bar.

Or, not so much the bar as the complete lack of anyone behind it.

And yet, the drinks were still being made. Right there, right now, with her very own eyes she could see the shaker sloshing up and down, the cap twisting off, clear liquid pouring out into a martini glass, an olive landing—plink!—in the v of the glass and nestling in to stay.

What the heck?

Denali had said he had something special to show her, but she'd assumed that would end like it always did: him trolling her with some ridiculous internet meme on his phone.

Indra peered closer in the dim light.

She blinked, eyes widening.

The fairy lights were not fairylights.

Well, they were not fairy lights in that they were not small LEDs strung together on a plastic-coated wire for the purpose of atmosphere and decoration.

They were, however, *fairy*-pause-*lights*: tiny people-shaped creatures no taller than Indra's fingers, complete with the stereotypical butterfly wings and slightly ragged slips of clothing, glowing blue in the night.

Indra shivered, and not only because another gust of salt-laden air washed coolly over the backyard.

In the corner of her eyes, the palm trees waved. She spun toward them. But they were only plastic inflatables, five-foot high and shining in the reflected light from the back patio—not twenty-foot plants with huge, frondy leaves, as they had appeared for a moment.

Indra shook her head a little and turned back to the bar. She frowned. The little fairies had to be a trick of some kind, one of Denali's quote 'master-pieces' that he was always bragging about.

Whatever. She could still have a drink, and in an hour she'd make her polite goodbyes and happy birthdays and leave for the magic of the beach at night.

But to get a drink… She pursed her lips. "How does this even work?"

Denali appeared beside her, as if out of thin air, laughing so his dark eyes twinkled with blue fairy light, his dark hair a shock of shadow in the night. "Do you like it?" he said, spinning in a circle with his arms out wide.

Drunk.

Clearly drunk, though she couldn't smell the alcohol on him.

He laughed again. "Tell it what you want," he said, and leaned toward her eagerly.

"Lemon lime and bitters?" Indra shrugged.

"No, no, no." Denali waved a hand at her, much too steadily considering how far gone he seemed to be. "Not to *drink*. Where you want to *go*. What you want to *do*. Who you want to *be*."

That was an awful lot of philosophy for nine p.m. on a Saturday night with a full moon.

"Do I have to answer all three?"

The first would be simple. The third? Question-able. At this point, she could only speculate on the answer. After all, did *anyone* know what they wanted to be?

Denali laughed as though no other reaction was possible, as though what he was drunk on was not alcohol, but delight, as though the sound bubbling out from him was pure, unadulterated joy.

Abruptly, Indra realised that Denali wasn't the only one laughing like that.

She squinted at the bar. "What are you spiking it with?"

Denali took her hand, grinning—without laughing, thank dog. "Indra. No spiking. I promise." He laid her hand against his heart, teeth so white they gleamed blue in the fairy light. "Trust me?"

Indra snorted. "Five times," she said, narrowing her eyes at him. "Five times, and every bloody time it was that stupid meme."

Denali looked thoughtful. "True. Okay. Fair." He released her hand. "Don't trust me then," he said, and began backing away, grin once more firmly in place. "Trust them." He tilted his head at the bar.

Indra turned, saw nothing, turned back—and Denali was gone, vanished somewhere into the dark of the buzzing crowd.

Trust who? What the hell?

Sighing, blinking, shaking her head, she leaned her elbows back on the bar and resigned herself to counting away the remaining—she checked her phone—forty-one minutes.

Salt air breathed over her face.

She closed her eyes, inhaling.

Forty minutes. Then she could go pretend there was magic in the world, that all the broken pieces of her life didn't matter, that somehow, everything would be okay.

That hot, tickling, prickling sensation began in the corners of her eyes, her throat constricting.

No.

The beach. If she could just make it to the beach, she'd forget about the rest of her life, and things would be fine.

Where did she want to go? The beach.

What did she want to do? Stop thinking about her parents' impending divorce, and her failed university subjects.

Who did she want to be? Someone at the beach, not thinking about anything but the possibility of magic in the world.

Silvered waves, cresting into foam, shushing against the shore. The dark horizon, endless and finite all at the same time. Silver face of the moon, ying and yang, dark and light, shadow and white. Cold sand between her toes, a strand of beach grass thick and rough between her fingertips. Salt breeze on her nose, her lips, her cheeks, the tickling as her hair whipped lightly at her face.

Indra inhaled deeply—and the salt smell was so strong, she opened her eyes.

And froze.

She couldn't be at the beach. She *couldn't*.

If she strained her ears, she could even hear the thrumming baseline of the party still. So what was this? Some kind of intense hallucination?

Her heart skipped. Denali had said he hadn't spiked the drinks but this was strange, too strange, this wasn't her imagination and maybe he'd been smoking something, and she'd inhaled too deeply and been caught in his haze…

Indra forced herself to take several calming breaths—even if they were slightly shallow, just in case—and told herself sternly to calm-the-heck down.

Her pulse disagreed vehemently, still sprinting for the wire—and nearly bursting right out of her ribcage as something blue and glowing landed softly on her shoulder, like a bird.

"It's alright," the fairy said. "You are quite well."

It was challenging to stare wide-eyed at a creature only a few inches tall on your own shoulder, but Indra managed it skilfully.

"I am not a hallucination," the creature said, shaking its head. "Yes, I know I might still say that even if I were a hallucination." The gender-indeterminate fairy smiled wryly from under a shock of blue hair. "I assure you, I am not."

Indra tried to speak—failed—wet her lips—tried again. "Then... why can't everyone else see... this?" She waved at the ocean, still shushing away in front of her.

"Because," said the fairy gently, "our job at the party tonight is to transport you to where you wish to be."

"But the others..."

"...wish to be at some grander sort of version of their party. You wish to be alone, and dreaming of magic." The fairy shrugged.

"But I didn't drink anything. Or ask for anything."

The fairy's smile this time was impish, delighted. "You were projecting your desires so strongly, you didn't need to verbalise them. Feeling somewhat... *sympathetic* to your desires, I thought perhaps I might give you a hand *without* the need for a conduit."

Indra blinked, thinking that one through. "You... don't want to be here either?"

The fairy's delight deepened. "Do any of us?" They vanished, their light winking out like a star.

Indra exhaled.

On the one hand, she could probably request her way back to reality. Back to the yard, with its bar and pounding basslines and clouds of cheap perfume and sweat—and people imagining they were elsewhere. Imagining very *intensely*, from the sound of it.

She glanced around. And *effectively*. With help.

Her lips twitched.

On the other hand, she was still at the party, wasn't she? Just like she'd promised? And Denali would no doubt be delighted that she was making full use of his party trick.

Smiling, tension draining from her shoulders, Indra angled herself so she could see the moon, and sat down in the cool, soft sand.

Forty minutes, or thirty-nine, or thirty-eight... Honestly, it probably didn't matter anymore.

One Fey, One Thief, One Dragon

THE SWEET STENCH OF WEED FILLED JASMARI'S NOStrils and her upper lip curled. On the main dance floor, wreathed in neon and shadow, the mortals pulsed to the clashing din they called music. If they but knew who she was that stood among them, they would tremble, as well they ought.

Instead, Jasmari kept her glamour firmly in place and followed Nate's slight form as he wound through the almost tangible cloud of cheap perfume and smoke and sweat to a stairwell, painted entirely in the matte black of the dance club itself.

Her glamour, of course, was barely necessary, with the mortals as distracted as they were, but there were appearances to consider. Literally.

Jasmari allowed herself an undignified snort at the word play—and paused with her hand on the smooth, cold rail of the stairs, head tilted.

Another fey was here.

She ran her tongue over the back of her sharp-pointed teeth.

"Problem?" Nate turned, midway up the first flight of stairs, and in the dim blue light one brow lifted.

Jasmari smiled, pointed teeth showing. "Why would there be trouble?"

'Nothing I can't handle' would also have been an acceptable reply, because when Jasmari found out who had been stupid enough to come here—besides herself, obviously, she really should have charged triple—they would be a problem no longer. Nor would they be much of anything else.

Nate turned away. Resumed climbing the stairs, footsteps echoing down the narrow, poorly lit hall that stretched to their left.

Jasmari nearly ignored the movement in the corner of her eye, the glimpse of glamour at the far end of that hall—

But an alarm pierced the air, pierced her ears, pierced her head, and she was cradling her temples in her hands wishing the pain would stop, doubling over, retching…

Nate laid a hand on her shoulder.

Jasmari slapped it away, inhaling deeply. He was lucky that looks couldn't kill, because then no one could blame her if he fell down dead.

He bowed his head, accepting the reprimand for touching her.

Through the pain, Jasmari bared her teeth. His bow had been barely more than a long-held nod, a gesture of respect between two equals, and he was no equal of hers, this pipsqueak of a man who thought himself so clever, so important, because he ran this, this, *establishment*.

"I'll go turn it off," Nate said simply, and vanished up the stairs.

For a brief moment, Jasmari considered following—but the alarm still blared, screeching through her defences and leaving her dazed and pained.

She swore. Where had Nate gotten a fey alarm from? Why hadn't Antiqua warned her?

And—she swore again—who was the other fey here, the one stupid enough to have set off the alarm in the first place?

She had a minute or two before Nate would return, she was sure of it. He *probably* hadn't set the alarm off deliberately, but he'd certainly be in no rush to turn it off before he saw how she bore up under it.

Jasmari would die before showing him weakness—and she couldn't die easily.

Breathing. Oxygen. It's only pain.

Exquisite, agonising fire burned through her head—but Jasmari was no stranger to pain. Slowly, slowly, she unbowed herself, set her shoulders, ground her teeth.

The end of the hall was twenty steps away, give or take.

And crumbled on the floor in the corner was a body, probably; difficult to be certain in the poor light—more of a glow than a light, a faint halo around the edges of objects like the pain was a halo around her thoughts.

Jasmari tossed her head.

That hurt.

But she refused to wince. And one step at a time, in a manner both studied and stately, Jasmari made it to the end of the hallway.

Akash sat crumpled on the floor.

Jasmari hissed. She'd kick him—pleasure surged through her chest at the thought—but it wouldn't break through the pain the alarm was causing.

Then he lifted his head.

Jasmari flinched away from the fierce eye contact, because she hadn't expected him—*him*, of all—to have carried away a dragon. But the shimmering green iridescence in his eyes was unmistakeable. "You fool," she whispered. "You have stolen one, and in doing so prevented me from freeing them all."

Akash bared his teeth in response, raising his wrist to her.

An iridescent green dragon writhed and romped around the dark skin of his arm like an animate tattoo, glittering in the dim light. It bared its teeth too, shook out the mane of elongated scales around its face, roared…

And Jasmari's stomach twisted at the flare of power the dragon sent out. Longing curled around her, desperate need for the power of the little dragon. She hadn't expected to actually *see* one on this visit; the best she'd been hoping for was some information about where they were kept, a hint as to where to concentrate their attack when finally Antiqua sent them to fetch the dragons back for good.

And Akash had freed one.

Jasmari ran her tongue along the pointed edges of her teeth.

The alarm cut off.

Nate.

Jasmari's gaze flickered between the stairs and the dragon on Akash's proffered arm. Back, forth, back, forth. If she ignored Akash, if she went with Nate, she might negotiate the release of all the dragons. At the very least she'd have information for Antiqua, and they could plan.

But Akash would no doubt be harmed.

Not from the humans, of course; they couldn't spot a fey who didn't want to be seen with a gilded map and a magic compass. Hence the need for their alarm.

But Antiqua would not be pleased.

And there was nothing to say that Nate was genuinely willing to barter; he loved a game as much as any of the fey. After all, he'd taken his sweet time in turning off the fey alarm, knowing all the while how much it was paining her.

One dragon, many dragons. Jasmari's fingers rippled against her elbow, once, twice, as she considered.

Nate's voice echoed in the hallway. "Your Highness?"

Jasmari sighed. "You fool," she said to Akash, but this time there wasn't any heat, because she was staring at the deep green dragon as though enchanted, and she knew she wouldn't have done any different had she seen one of them locked up.

Akash was scrambling back to his feet now the alarm had stopped. "Not a fool," he said coldly. "War is coming. They will not negotiate for the dragons, and you know it."

Mm. He was right, of course. All pretences aside, war was coming—and perhaps it was good for it to begin with a dragon on their side.

It was a simple matter to cast a deeper glamour over both of them—they would have seemed to disappear to mortal eyes—and Jasmari exhaled as the sweat-and-smoke smell of the club was shut away, already rehearsing what she would tell Antiqua.

Akash raised his eyebrows.

Jasmari ignored his surprise.

Under the shelter of the heavy glamour, they strode invisibly to the newly installed door, a gap in the heavy layers of wards that protected the building from the fey. As they stepped through easily to the little stairwell outside, Jasmari took a brief moment to wonder who's side Nate was really on.

And then she cast the charm and they vanished, one fey, one thief, and one dragon.

Cerulean Blue

ABANDONED SHIPS ALWAYS STANK OF METAL AND space dust, even through the spacesuit's copious filters. Celtahn wrinkled his nose—and tensed as the sound of movement came from ahead. He'd been the first onto the ship, and everyone else was behind him—weren't they?

The question was, had someone snuck in from behind and beaten him to the salvage? Or… was the ship not really dead at all?

Celtahn swallowed, the taste of metal thick on his tongue—black night, why did old ships have to taste so much like blood?—and stepped onward, mentally batting away stories and rumours that had been collecting in the dusty corners of his brain for years, stories of zombie ships crewed by a single person, ships that should have been dead, but that somehow clung to life instead, appearing where they were least expected, vanishing without explanation—and leaving a trail of death and mourning in their red-lit wake.

"Left ahead," his second-in-command breathed through the intercom.

The noise that had given Celthan pause had come from straight ahead down the dull grey corridor.

If it had even been a noise. If it hadn't just been the ship settling, or some old wreckage shifting. There was a reason he was here for salvage, after all.

So he turned left, because that was the way to the command centre, and even if someone else was here, if he reached the command centre unchallenged, he could always claim ignorance, and by then it would be too late to stop him because his crew would have the controls and the ship would be theirs, and...

He was babbling. Celtahn winced and straightened.

Zombie ships weren't real. This was ridiculous.

A clang rang out from behind.

Celtahn whipped around—and so did the rest of the crew, staring at the grey, featureless t-junction where they'd just turned.

He'd be lying if he didn't admit that his hands were sweaty, his heart racing—but Celtahn swallowed that down, adjusted his blaster, and crept toward the junction regardless.

His second hissed as he went passed, made to grab at his wrist.

Celtahn shook him off.

At the corner, red light flared, a sparkling, shimmering burst from the left that was there and then gone, like nothing he'd ever seen before.

Red.

That… That was not good.

If it had been blue, or even green or purple, it would have meant Clan magic. But red? With that kind of sparkle? That meant foreign magic—and suddenly the stories of zombie ships made a jot more sense.

Of course you couldn't solo-pilot a ship with Clan magic. But with something else?

No wonder the viciously xenophobic Clans called them zombies, perpetuated stories that would result in their deaths.

Heart still walloping away in his ears, Celtahn edged closer to the corner. He wrinkled his nose at the sudden scent of flowers—a sure sign of a magical discharge.

"Hello?" he called, suit projecting his voice out into the atmosphere of the ship. "Who's there? Show yourself."

His voiced sounded confident, sure, and he was glad.

A scuffle.

He shifted his grip on his blaster. "Come out! This is Salvage Crew 3-9-6 Alpha Rose, of Clan

Azure. We're armed, and here for salvage. You won't be harmed if you cooperate."

A noise that sounded distinctly like a sigh—and then a hand appeared around the corner of the grey wall.

"Actually," said a female voice, "let's flip that. This is Salvage Crew 6-7-1 Beta Lily, Clan Cerulean. And we were here first."

The rest of the woman appeared around the corner, following the hand. She'd taken the helmet of her suit off—a soft grey that blended with the walls, though Celtahn could see at a glance the mended patches on her thigh and left bicep—and her face stopped Celtahn in his tracks.

He couldn't have said, right at that moment, whether it was because she was gorgeous, or terrifying. Possibly both.

Then he realised she'd said Clan Cerulean, and snapped his mental shields into place to protect himself from any undue mind influence she might be exerting.

Oddly enough, she was still both beautiful and terrifying, dark hair pulled back into a pony tail, dark eyes flashing—and the faintest, barely visible glow of red around her left hand.

Celtahn took a step back.

"Great." The woman beamed an award-worthy smile at him, one hip cocked. "I take it you're retreating then, and happy to concede our prior claim to salvage." Bright blue light played over her fingers as she rippled them in the air.

Not red.

Not even purple.

Bright, rich, cerulean blue.

Celtahn inhaled slowly. It was simpler to believe that she'd been using her mind control powers just before, making the light *appear* red, when really it was blue.

And sometimes, the simplest answer was the best one.

No matter what the truth was.

Celtahn beamed back a grin of his own, one he knew from experience never failed to get him what he wanted. "Tell you what," he said. "Why don't we call it a joint salvage? Split the profits, sixty-forty."

The woman arched an eyebrow. "Sixty to me, I assume, since my crew found it first."

Celtahn kept the grin going.

The woman bit briefly at her lip, as though trying to keep her earlier smile from returning to her face. "Fine. Fifty-fifty. She's a big ship, and my crew would appreciate the help. We're only a little tug." She gave a small shake of her head, as though she couldn't believe what she was hearing herself say.

"Fifty-fifty," Celtahn said, still grinning the grin that was yet to ever fail him.

"Come on," she said, tossing her head and indicating the corridor she'd appeared from. "I know the maps say the command room is that way, but they changed up the layout. I'll take you there." She disappeared back around the corner.

"You going to trust her?" Celtahn's second whispered at him.

He stared at the empty junction.

It couldn't have been red light he'd seen.

And zombie ships weren't really real. Just a story made up by social influencers to keep the masses steady. He'd been part of enough whisper campaigns himself to believe that in his heart of hearts, no matter what his fears might mutter.

"Yeah," he said, nodding. "I'm going to trust her."

And so he rounded the corner in the dead, dusty ship, with the taste of metal heavy on his tongue. Someone had beaten him to the salvage after all, but right now, as the woman paused and smiled back when she heard him following, he couldn't quite bring himself to mind.

ABOUT THE AUTHOR

AMY LAURENS is an award-winning Australian author of fantasy and science fiction for both adults and young adults.

She has written the award-winning portal-fantasy *Sanctuary* series about Edge, a 13-year-old girl forced to move to a small country town due to witness protection (the first book is *Where Shadows Rise*), the humorous fantasy *Kaditeos* series, following newly-graduated Evil Overlord Mercury as she attempts to acquire a castle, the young adult *Storm Foxes* series about love and magic and mental health, and a whole host of non-fiction, usually about dogs and writing.

You can find out more at
www.amylaurens.com.

Read more by Amy Laurens!

HOW NOT TO ACQUIRE A CASTLE

On a hard plastic chair in the front row of the Great Hall in the world's fifth-best Evil Overlording Academy, with its red-wooden parquetry floor that spoke of wealth and the beige, square panels of sound-boards speaking of conservatism on the walls, Mercury sat, pointedly not sweating.

Partly, this was because the Academy Administrators had deigned to turn on the air-conditioning earlier in the day, in recognition of the fact that the hall would be packed out with approximately six hundred bodies, all here to celebrate the graduation of about a third of that crowd.

But mostly, Mercury was pointedly not sweating because she made it a point never to sweat, sweat being an indication that she was working hard, and hard work being antithetical to her way of life.

However. If she *had* been sweating right now, it would not have been due to the uncomfortable warmth of six hundred packed bodies that even the air-conditioning system couldn't completely shift, or, in fact, from over-exertion. Instead, it would have been caused by an even more unfamiliar concept in Mercury's emotional vocabulary: nervousness.

Mercury did not *get* nervous. Mercury got things *done*.

So the fact that she was sitting here, in the front row of the Great Hall, about to graduate from Evil Overlording Academy (with distinction), and was feeling *nervous*... She crumpled the black paper program in her pale fists. It made her furious, that's what it did. Abjectly furious, that snooty-tooty Deviran with his stupid morals and his stupid I-don't-want-to-be-here and his stupid Overlords-are-empty-figureheads and his stupid face sitting ten people over, looking implacable with his deep brown skin and barely-there, precision-groomed beard, as though he knew it gave him a stupid air of alluringly stupid mystery...

Mercury scowled and searched for the train of thought that had been derailed, yet again, by Deviran's stupidity.

Ah. Yes. She was angry because she was nervous because she wasn't absolutely entirely one hundred and fifty percent sure that she'd beaten Deviran in their final exams, and 1) being anything less than a hundred and fifty percent certain of anything made her cranky, and 2) being beaten by Deviran for dux of the year would be utterly unbearable. She flicked away a piece of fluff that had become snagged under her immaculately magenta-painted nails and smoothed out the black paper program.

In the front corner of the hall, the starkly-attired string quartet with their traditional black instruments began playing the March of the Oncoming Doom. The screechy scrapes of hundreds of chairs on the hall's wooden floor sounded as the crowd climbed to its collective feet.

Mercury sat with her arms firmly folded for a few moments longer, until her best friend Sparky kicked her in the ankle.

"Get up, idiot," Sparky hissed, hints of real flame flickering through her flame-coloured pixie cut.

"No," Mercury said, flouncing to her feet and tossing her own glossy brown hair back over her shoulders. Four years she'd been playing by the Academy's rules in order to get what she wanted, and she'd had just about enough. Other people's rules should only be applied to plebs too stupid to invent their own.

Sparky rolled her eyes somewhere over Mercury's head before focusing on the stage, where the ceremonial party had begun entering.

Mercury clenched her jaw and narrowed her own eyes as the teachers of the Evil Overlording Academy filed onto the stage, dressed in their formal finery. Each teacher had their own distinctive look that matched their personality and their Overlording style, from severe charcoal suits to jet-black leathers, pastel ballgowns and gem-toned lingerie and eye-blinding spandex, and even on one tiny old woman at the back, worn jeans and a grey flannel shirt. She was the one to watch out for, of course; Mercury could respect an Overlord who was confident enough in their abilities that they didn't need to telegraph them. It wasn't a look *she* would consider, of course, but still. She could respect it.

The band's march finished and, after a moderately awkward pause, the crowd sat. The Principal, pale skin and dark hair matching his suspiciously vampiric red-and-black suit, took the podium, and Mercury narrowed her eyes. He was doing a superb job of hiding his emotions—he was a premier Evil Overlord, after all—but she was Mercury, and unlike anyone else, she had the benefit of being able to rummage through people's consciousnesses. She was better at adding things *into* people's minds than taking information out, but he was telegraphing fear loudly enough that she could sense it without trying overly much.

Mercury pursed her lips. Hmm.

The Principal cleared his throat at the blackened-wood podium, and the fear made it into his usually-unreadable eyes. "Before we begin," he said, and Mercury's stomach did a peculiar kind of flip-flop. "I have a pressing announcement to make regarding the safety of our students and their families." He cleared his throat again and took out a sheet of paper from his pocket, unfolding it carefully and smoothing out the creases before beginning again. "The Council"—quiet booing echoed around the hall, and Mercury tsked impatiently—"have asked me to recommend that students from Tumul Tuos seriously consider postponing their return to town for a few days. The city is dealing with a *situation* at present which may present a danger to our students' health and safety."

Mercury's hands fisted at her sides and she forced herself to remain seated. What was wrong with her city? What had the Council mucked up now? A risk to the students' safety? There had to be more he wasn't telling them. Gently, Mercury tugged on his consciousness, implanting the suggestion that it might be better to share the news than to keep it secret. After all, how could they fight an enemy they didn't know?

"There are, ah..." He trailed off, glancing side to side as though wondering why his mouth had decided to continue.

Mercury didn't snicker, but she did press her lips together in satisfaction.

The Principal took a deep, steadying breath and seemed to change tack. "There has been one death already. The family have already been notified, so it is with much regret that I must inform you that Woovermyer will no longer be with us at the Evil Overlording Academy."

Murmurs broke out around the room, not all of them sad—to be expected in a school devoted to raising the next generation of dictators (ish) and despots (of sorts).

Mercury, however, crushed her program in her left hand, fist so tight her nails bit her palm.

"You okay?" Sparky murmured, leaning toward her.

Mercury gave a single, tense shake of her head and stared at the podium. Dead. Livie Woovermyer was dead in *her city*. And the Council hadn't done anything to stop it. Couldn't do anything to stop it, probably, given they'd warned the students to stay away. Livie hadn't been the strongest candidate in the year level, but she was no lightweight, either. It would take a lot of power to kill a Seven.

Enough was enough.

A good thing Mercury was about to graduate at the top of the class, giving her the right to knock the lowest ranking current Overord off their perch. Tumul Tuos would be hers in a matter of hours. And then there'd be no more of these wasteful deaths. Her city would be safe at last.

Madame Pompadour was up the front now, elbow gloves the same glimmery silver colour as her elaborate, piled-curls wig, eyelids gleaming with matching silver eye shadow, and abruptly Mercury realised Madame was there to make the announcement that would change her life forever.

She leaned forward in her seat, ready to stand when her name was called.

"And now the announcement you've all been dying for," the Political Alliances teacher trilled, the frills on her evening gown fluttering as she moved. "The dux of this year's cohort!"

Sweat slicked Mercury's palms. Irritated, she reached over and wiped them on Sparky's thigh.

Sparky pushed Mercury's hands back into her own personal space bubble and Mercury, nervous to the edge of distraction, let her.

"Will you please join me in welcoming to the stage, our wonderful dux for this year, Deviran Goodsmith!"

Mercury froze halfway to standing. "Did she just say Deviran?" she whispered furiously to Sparky.

Sparky hauled her forcibly back down into her seat. "Yes," she hissed back. "Sit down, you're making a fool of yourself."

Mercury's spine snapped upright as she sat, and she arranged the folds of her long black skirt demurely. "No I'm not." She closed her eyes. "Deviran's going up to the stage, isn't he?" Even at a whisper, the misery in her voice was clear, but this time, she didn't care.

Sparky reached over and squeezed her hand.

Mercury squeezed back, lacing her fingers back through Sparky's, and held tight as all her plans and dreams vanished in front of her.

A stone had landed in her chest. That must be it. Some strange sort of magic that made her chest contract and sink, and made the world distort for just a moment, long enough to trick her into thinking Deviran had beaten her so that someone could jump in front of her and yell SURPRISE!

Any moment now.

Any moment.

She refused to open her eyes and watch Deviran parading across the stupid stage like some stupid stupid-person, receiving his stupid medal and stupid symbolic crest pin.

It was that last exam question. She'd known Deviran would pull out his ridiculous 'Evil Overlords are merely figureheads, the Business Guild is where the power really lies' rant that everyone had heard a million times back when he was younger and angrier, and she'd tried to counter it, she really had.

She'd argued for the importance of the Overlording position, for the power of having a symbolic figure to unite the population in their hatred, for having a person able to make all the difficult, necessary decisions the Council was too weak and spineless to make... But it hadn't been enough.

Everything she'd worked for, everything she'd set out to prove—and it wasn't enough.

There were words, there were names, and then forever later, once she'd died twice already, Sparky elbowed her in the ribs. "Come on," Sparky muttered. "We're up next."

And sure enough, there was a shuffling of presenters as the last of the Powers Behind The Throne graduates departed the stage, and the next speaker announced in threatening, funereal tones, "The Overlording cohort."

Mercury blinked furiously and followed Sparky to the end of the line at the right side of the stage. The other candidates proceeded one at a time across the stage, two girls and then stupid Deviran, and then a handful more and then Sparky, and then the speaker was calling her name.

Hands fisted, Mercury tossed her head high, climbed the four steps, and marched across the stage. She wouldn't look at them, the stupid faculty who'd denied her the city she rightfully deserved, and she wouldn't look the other way either, at the classmates and crowd undoubtedly sniggering at her failure.

She shook hands with the presenter, and while he pinned the tiny crossed-swords badge on her collar, her eyes betrayed her and slid toward the audience. Her stomach flipped as she saw the crowd of parents and friends behind the rows of students, all the way to the back of the hall, twenty rows at least, illuminated by the late afternoon light streaming in through the ceiling-high windows to the right. Everyone had someone here to watch them graduate. Everyone except Weird Al—and her.

The presenter finished with her pin, muttered something to her, and offered his hand again. Mercury coldly ignored it and strode from the stage. It didn't matter. None of it mattered. Tumul Tuos was her city anyway, and no one could change that. She'd think of something. She'd take a day or two out, make some plans...

And she could always hope that Deviran would choose some other Overlording territory. He'd be stupid to, but then again, he was stupid, so. Mercury could hope.

All at once, mid-way down the steps off the stage, Mercury came to rigid attention, scanning the room.

Somewhere out there in the crowd, an exchange of power had just taken place, and it felt... unusual.

But the final few students were backing up behind her and muttering, so Mercury headed back toward her seat, craning her head all the while and searching for some sign of whatever it was that had just discharged a dizzyingly quiet amount of power into the room.

She sat, and Sparky leaned over. "Okay?"

"Mm," said Mercury. "Did you feel…" She accidentally caught the eye of the student behind her and twisted back to face the front.

"Feel what?"

Mercury turned it over in her mind. It had felt like a large shot of power discharged very quietly—but perhaps it hadn't been. Perhaps it had only been a small discharge after all, something most people wouldn't have noticed.

But still, something about it had tugged on her. It very nearly felt like something she'd felt before, only she *knew* she'd never sensed that kind of discharge. She shook her head. "Never mind. Don't worry."

Sparky sighed and straightened. "It's fine, Mercury," she said, drily exasperated. "I know you didn't win, but I promise, you'll live through it."

Mercury waved a hand for silence.

The power had just discharged again, and it had come from somewhere in the back corner, far away from the windows and light.

Impatiently, Mercury waited for the formalities to conclude. The crowd stood while the quartet played the exit march, and the stage party left, Mercury tapping her foot all the while.

The moment the last notes of the march died away, Mercury turned and headed to the back corner, weaving in and out of the students and parents who had seemed to explode slowly but inexorably out from the neat rows of seating, ignoring Sparky's calls behind her. Power, something that tugged in a way that was strange and familiar, all at once. She pushed her way through a family posing for pictures—and halted.

In the shadows of the back corner, Deviran stood with his family, with his stupid, smug little smile, looking as tall and dark and stupidly alluring as ever. Prat.

His mother, short but sleek, and his father—tall, and utterly terrifying in a way not at all diminished by his gleaming smile—gushed over him, patting his back and hugging him tight. Within moments the Principal was there, glibly shaking hands and congratulating them on the success of their son. Something flickered across his consciousness, and also Deviran's father's—some moment of recognition in response to what they were saying. But Mercury brushed it aside just as the mother brushed melodramatic tears from her cheeks and handed Deviran a silver-wrapped package about as long as her hand but half the width.

That. That was the source of the strange, magical feeling. Mercury watched hawk-eyed as Deviran unwrapped the gift. A glimpse of gold set her pulse racing—What was it? What did it do? Could she steal it?—and then the paper fell away to the floor, and Deviran stood staring wordlessly at the object in his hands, and Mercury did too.

Wide-eyed, Deviran raised his gaze to his parents, and even from where she stood Mercury could hear the reverence in his voice as he thanked them.

But Mercury had eyes only for the object. No wonder she'd felt it discharge, and no wonder it had felt both strange and familiar. In Deviran's hands lay a glorious, sunshine-gold key, large and strong—and with a handle in the shape of a stylised fish, long, flowing fins curving to make the grip.

A Key. They'd given him a Key. And not just any Key, but *the* Key, *her* Key, the Artefact of Power belonging to *her* city.

A wordless noise of wanting rose in Mercury's throat. Who cared about being dux? She needed that Key.

Keep reading! Head to
https://www.amylaurens.com/books/
kaditeos/castle/
to buy your copy now!